Snowed

A Sierra Hockey Novella

Elise Faber

SNOWED
BY ELISE FABER

Newsletter sign-up

SIERRA HOCKEY SERIES

ONE

JOLIE

The music is so loud it's giving me a headache.

Pulsing and mixing with the flashing lights and making me grumpier than I already am.

Mostly because I don't want to be out.

I want to be in bed, cuddled in my velvet jammies, drinking the frothy hot chocolate from the special mix I treat myself to during this time of year. In fact, I bought myself an extra box knowing this month was coming.

December.

Hellish.

Busy.

Full to the brim with *Christmas*.

Yes, I say that in my head like it's a four-letter word.

Smothering a sigh, I rub my temple, fighting the headache brewing there, knowing I'm just tired and cranky because I worked all day. Again. Knowing that I'm *extra* tired after busting my ass for weeks on end, pulling eighty-hour weeks because everyone waits until the last minute to get ready for the holidays.

And as a hairstylist, that means the last month has been filled with cuts and freshening up colors and doing styles for *so* many holiday parties. Add in listening to all the drama that everyone inevitably fills my ears with, decorating my own place, and doing my own shopping, and...I do not want to be here right now.

I want velvet jammies and hot cocoa and to sleep for a hundred years.

But Toby wanted to try this new club. And so did Colleen.

And when my boyfriend and best friend want something, I'm overruled.

Hence, the reason my ass is currently parked on a barstool, club music assaulting my ears and the flashing lights from the dance floor making my eyes hurt.

"And then," Colleen says, her gorgeous lips curved in a smile, "I went to my boss and..."

She leans closer to Toby, finishing a story I can't hear over the din—or maybe I can't hear it because I'm the aforementioned tired and not listening all that well.

Either way, she stops talking and Toby bursts out laughing, and I slug back the remnants of my drink.

"Be right back," I tell them, hopping off my stool and snagging my purse.

"You good, babe?" Colleen asks.

"Bathroom," I shout over the sound of the music before taking off for the bathroom.

Bracing myself, I weave my way through the throng of bodies, pushing beyond the crush and making it to the hallway. Thankfully, it's quieter in the hall, and I lean back against the wall and take a breath, trying to summon the fun Jolie.

Unfortunately, I think she's gone south for the winter.

Or maybe she's gone forever.

Run out of town by bills and adult responsibilities and just feeling *tired*, all the freaking time.

Sighing, I push off the wall, start to head to the bathroom. If I'm out—and not in my comfy jammies—I should make the best of it. Get another drink, take some silly pictures with Colleen and Toby. Maybe make a TikTok and—

I pat my pockets.

"Shit," I mutter, realizing I left my cell on the bar top.

Normally, I would just use the bathroom then go back for it. But it's a brand-new phone because I dunked my old one in a sink while washing the toner out of a client's hair a few days ago, and I barely got this new one set up in the subsequent chaos of my work week.

I don't want to risk it getting stolen or a drink spilled on it or—

I just don't want to risk it, okay?

Preparing myself for the noise, I turn around and move back into the throng of writhing bodies, expecting to have to push and shove my way through again.

Only this time, it's like the crowd is the Red Sea.

They part before me, leaving an opening I can easily walk through.

But just as I start to do that, some instinct inside prompts me to look up.

To stare across the open space.

To look toward the trio of stools where I'd just been sitting.

They're empty.

No, only *two* of them are empty. One is occupied. By Toby... and Colleen. They're wrapped in each other's arms, mouths pressed together, and—

I stumble as someone bumps into me.

Toby's hands are on Colleen's ass, dipping under the short hem of her bodycon dress, rubbing lightly across the backs of her thighs.

I like that.

That is my favorite thing Toby does. A little tease. A little naughty. *Mine.*

Only, he's doing it to my best friend.

Someone bumps into me again, harder this time, and I don't know if the contact just catches me wrong or my legs are weak because of the scene I'm trying to process in front of me. The only thing I *do* process is that I'm flying through the air, landing hard on my knees.

Pain shooting up my legs.

My palms scrape against the floor, sending a burning heat through my arms.

Someone steps on my hand, and I cry out, jerking back, holding it to my chest, watching them kiss and kiss and *kiss.*

Watching my cell sitting there on the table, sad and unattended and...

Scooped up by someone brushing by them.

There and gone in a second.

I shove to my feet, intending to go after the man who is currently walking away, shoving my phone into his pocket. But I barely make it before I'm bumped again. This time, I tumble into a group of men, bouncing off them almost comically, seeing the floor flying up toward my face.

I brace for the impact—

And it doesn't come.

Instead, a big, warm hand wraps around my arm, catching me, hauling me back up to my feet. "Whoa," the rough voice says as he steadies me. "Easy there, sweetheart."

Sweetheart.

Normally, I hate the endearment, but in the husky voice that somehow reaches my ears over the cacophony of the club, it rolls like velvet over my skin.

Lifting goose bumps.

Sending a bolt of heat through my middle.

I spin, look up, up, *up*...into the prettiest pair of hazel eyes I've ever seen. Then stick my hand out and blurt, "My phone."

Those eyes go from mine to where I'm pointing.

"My boyfriend—" I clear my throat when his eyes come back. "He's supposed to watch it, watch out for my stuff, but he's—"

Those hazel eyes change, and I don't want to look too closely.

Don't want to see pity in the pretty golden-green depths.

"The guy in the red hat took it off the bar top," I say.

Another glance away and I watch his eyes narrow, the action drawing my focus to his thick lashes before he nods at someone next to him. "Lake?"

"On it," comes another voice, and I feel someone move away from the circle of men I'd toppled into, watch as he maneuvers through the crowd like he'd been born to navigate through tight spaces.

A hand drops to the side of my neck, squeezing lightly. "Your boyfriend?" tall, dark, and hazel-eyed asks softly.

Heat in my cheeks.

I try to pull back, but he doesn't let me, tugging me a little closer.

Near enough that I can see the intricate lines of a tattoo drifting above the neck of his T-shirt. Near enough I can smell the spicy scent of him.

"Your boyfriend?" he asks again.

I bite my lip. Release it.

Sigh softly because my eyes are welling up, and I really don't want to cry right now. "And my best friend," I say, glancing back at the bar, seeing them finally break apart, though they do it slowly, with lingering touches that have my stomach churning.

Colleen's lipstick isn't even messed up.

Christ, she even does make up better than me. My lipstick didn't make it beyond my first drink.

I need a drink.

About five of them.

The man curses, and I tear my eyes away from the stools of betrayal and look back up into those hazel eyes.

"Your best friend?" he repeats.

A tear spills over my lashes, and I tug at his hold. "I should go," I say. "I should—"

But I don't even get the rest of my protest out before he's moving me through the crowd, expertly navigating us so I don't get within an inch of another person, let alone get bumped again.

Then we're in the hall, and I'm still blinking from the sudden movement, from the guiding...

From the man pinning me to the wall and putting his scowling face in mine.

"Your boyfriend *and* your best friend?"

Two

Leo

I barely notice when Theo Young—the annoying fuck from the Breakers (and consequently not from *my* team, the Sierra, who are clearly superior)—follows Lake across the room, trailing after the asshole in the red hat who's trying to steal the woman's phone, leaving his half-drunk beer and unworn pair of Air Jordans on the table.

Long story.

Suffice to say Lake, my teammate and no doubt the face of the team (not to mention quite a few other products) did good shit talk.

It's why we're all here with the enemy.

Sharing a pitcher of beer.

But right now, that's the least of my concerns, especially with tears clinging to the lashes of the woman in front of me, her pale gray eyes swimming with pain, her color all wrong—too pink in some places, too pale in others.

I take her arm—narrowing my eyes at the group of team-mates who'd remained, silently telling them to mind their own fucking business and to not drink all of my beer. Something I knew they would ignore, just to fuck with me.

They are the only ones aside from Lake on the roster who I can actually stand (but that's a story for another time). Still, this is hockey.

Giving each other a hard time is a prerequisite.

Which is why I know my beer will be gone by the time I get back.

Normally, something I avoid at all costs.

Beer. Hockey. Food.

Priorities.

But this woman—

"I should go," she says so quietly that I have to strain to hear it. "I should—"

This woman, with those damp eyes and tears now sliding down her cheeks isn't a priority, but I can't ignore her, can't ignore the urge that I need to do something to make the hurt on her face go away. Can't ignore that I want to pull her close and hug her until she feels better.

Maybe it's the dark circles I can see in the flashing lights.

Maybe it's that wrong mix of pink and white on her face, like she's a dried-out leaf and just one false move away from crumpling.

Maybe it's the fact that she looks like she's willing to walk right out of this bar right now and never look back.

Never look back at *me*.

My throat tightens, and I take her arm and guide her out of the bar, out into the hallway, where it's quieter, where the light is steadier.

Drawing us to a halt, stepping close, and looking into those gorgeous gray eyes.

"Your boyfriend *and* your best friend?" I ask.

Her eyes close and she looks away, pain wracking her features, and I'm flooded with competing urges—to walk back across the dance floor and pound my fist in the fucker who *had been* (because that was order of business number one) this woman's boyfriend; to haul her close and give her that hug she clearly needs; and the one I give in to.

"Come on," I say softly, taking her hand this time and—

She cries out.

I freeze, the sound slicing through me.

The way she clutches her hand against her chest, cradling it carefully in the other *kills*.

Ignoring the guilt—for hurting her—and the worry— because these are big fucking feelings for a woman I met all of two minutes ago—I carefully wrap my arm around her shoulders and draw her forward.

Giving in to my final urge.

The one to take her out onto the back patio of the restaurant, the one that's closed because there's tons of snow on the ground from the winter's record-breaking snowfall. It's empty.

Private.

She shivers against me the moment the first blast of cool winter air hits.

Cold.

I drop my arm, hate that she shivers again, but I make it quick, peeling my jacket off my arms, wrapping it around her and tugging her close again, guiding her to a table that had been cleared of snow, nudging her down so she sits on one of the attached wooden benches.

"Let me see," I order gently, picking up her hand and angling it so I can study the bruise already blooming on the back of it, the way her fingers are swelling up.

Damn.

I wince. "You might need to get that X-rayed."

She jerks, hand yanking from mine as she makes another pained sound that grates at my soul. "No." A shake of her head pairs with tentative flexing of her hand, her jaw clenching as she tries to hide that it's clearly hurting. "See? It's fine."

I snort. "Yeah, sweetheart, that's not fine."

She can barely move her fingers.

She shakes her head again. "I have to work tomorrow."

Yeah, that isn't happening.

But I don't argue with her, just move a little closer. "What's your name?"

She freezes, dark brown hair sliding forward to cover her face.

And she has great *fucking* hair, shining in the moonlight, thick and full of curls that I want drifting over my naked skin.

Something *else* that isn't going to happen considering the fact that she's just caught her boyfriend and best friend kissing.

Kissing like they've been fucking.

Trust me, I know.

No man kisses a woman like that without—

She flexes her hand again and grimaces, and I stop thinking about the boyfriend and fucking and wanting to plow *my* hand into his face.

"What's your name?" I ask again.

Her head comes up. "Jolie."

Fucking perfect, that name for her. It sounds like it should belong to a rockstar, and paired with the kickass jeans, the necklaces, the fuck-me hair, and the curves for days, and Jolie is giving me rocker vibes.

Her brows flick up, the fragile disappearing, a bit of fire coming out.

And fuck, this isn't good.

For me.

For my head.

For...my heart.

"What?" I ask genuinely curious.

"You gonna tell me your name?" Her question is tart.

Nope. Definitely not good, but I still say, "I'm Leo."

"Huh." She keeps tentatively moving her fingers, her hand, my jacket still around her shoulders, still dwarfing her, but her gaze slides from mine, focuses to the side.

To the lake.

Moonlight glimmers over the soft waves as they break against the shore, darkening the beige sand, highlighting the snow piled up on the beach.

And she falls quiet.

"What?"

"Nothing," she says after a moment, gaze still in the distance. "Just that your name fits you." She exhales, glances back up at me, lips parting—

Just as the back door of the bar swings open.

Lake walks out, phone in his hand. "Here you go, sweetheart."

Jolie scowls, just for a second, and I can't lie. That makes a tiny blip of joy settle in my cold, dead heart. Every woman melts for Lake. Always.

Except...apparently, not Jolie.

Then her scowl smooths an instant later, and she takes it, holding it in her uninjured hand like it's the key to humanity. "Thank you," she says.

"No problem."

"Really"—she holds it closer—"you don't know how much this means to me. My whole life is on here."

Lake nods, bends a little to catch her eyes. "It's not a problem. Red Hat decided that it was easier to just give it to me rather than waiting for the sheriff."

"Thank you," she whispers again. "So, *so* much."

Lake squeezes her arm. "It's really okay. Hope your night gets better, yeah?"

She nods, and Lake turns away, slanting a glance at me as he walks back inside.

I know what that look means.

And I'm not looking forward to it.

"I need to go." Standing, Jolie starts to shrug my jacket off, that thread of fragile reappearing, drawing me toward her like a cat to a mouse.

I catch her...*and* the jacket, wrapping the latter around her before she can shiver again.

"What are you doing?" I ask.

Fragile disappears, and her chin comes up. "I'm going home," she snaps.

"Home?" My brows tick up, irritation making the word terse.

Pink on her cheeks. "Is that *okay* with you?"

My temper flares, and I step closer. "Going home *where?* With that asshole?"

Her eyebrows drag together, and I watch as she deflates slightly. "No. He and—" Here she falters, throat working. "Toby and Colleen came together," she whispers. "I met them after work." A sigh. "Makes sense why now." Another exhale. "I need to go home—*by myself*—because I have work in the morning."

Work.

Yeah, that isn't—

She's still clutching her phone. "Thanks for your help."

I watch her shoulders rise and fall again.

Slender. Fragile.

But there is steel beneath.

Beautiful, tempered steel.

She moves, slipping from the coat, and shoving it into my hands in one smooth movement. "Have a nice life, Leo."

Then she turns and walks away.

THREE

JOLIE

I reach for the door handle just as a hand drops onto my shoulder and I'm spun back around.

"Have a nice *life?*" Leo snaps.

"I—"

"Really?" he says, still snapping.

"I—" I blink, genuinely confused before reality hits. Of course. He did me a favor, retrieving my cell—or sending someone after it anyway—and now he wants... "Uh...do you want money for getting my phone?"

Which, right...

I glance down like my purse will magically transport itself from the bar next to Colleen and Toby and onto my shoulder.

In fairness—and lack of magical abilities aside—they're probably watching that about as well as they did my phone.

Which means I will have credit cards to cancel.

Though, what does that say about me that my worry for my cell was greater than it is for my purse? Probably because my life is in my phone, and while losing my purse would be inconvenient, losing my cell—

The door swings open again, narrowly missing us—the *narrowly* part coming because Leo jerks me out of the way.

"Fuck, Theo," Leo mutters. "What's your problem?"

The man—Theo, apparently—draws to a halt, his hand clamped over his heart. "Doors," he mutters. "Jesus Christ." Then he shakes his head. "Sorry. Here," he says, holding out my purse and my jacket, "I figured you'd need these."

"Oh," I murmur, disappointment settling heavily in my belly. Stupid, huh? "I guess Toby—"

Leo snorts.

I turn, lift my brows. "What?"

A shrug of those big, broad shoulders. "Toby is a dumbass name."

My brows lift higher, but I can't focus on that, not with Theo passing me my purse as I turn back. "He didn't notice?" I can't help but ask.

The expression on Theo's face tells me enough.

No.

Toby didn't notice my purse being picked up by a stranger, nor my jacket. The same as he didn't notice my cell making it into the pocket of Red Hat's jeans.

Too busy with Colleen.

Which...God, that really hurts.

"Thanks," I say instead of letting the pity on Theo's face slice me deeper.

"Honey," Theo begins.

Leo growls.

Theo's brows shoot up, gaze going over my shoulder, but then his expression relaxes, mouth tipping up.

I blink, shake off the melancholy, the confusion, the...mix of weirdness in my belly. Like even though my life has just imploded, I'm standing on the precipice of something...something big. "I—" I clamp my lips together, clear my throat, then exhale, shoving that all aside. "Just, thanks."

Theo nods, turns away with his lips still curved, and grabs the handle, slipping back in through the door, albeit much more cautiously this time.

The wooden and glass panel slams closed, and I ignore the throbbing in my hand as I reach my uninjured one into my purse, digging out my keys. Home, ice, ibuprofen, change the code on my smart lock (ensuring both Toby *and* Colleen can't get into my place), then sleep.

Tomorrow I'll work.

I'll ignore the hurt.

I'll break up with Toby...*and* Colleen.

Then I'll drink my frothy hot cocoa, slip into my expensive and cozy jam-jams, and sleep through the night, through the next day, because, thankfully, I take Sundays off.

Then...back to work.

Making money because I can't make my fucking love life work. Or friendships, apparently.

Right.

Not the time to think about that.

Home. Ibuprofen. Sleep.

Good plan.

"Jolie."

I shiver—not because I'm cold, but because his voice and my name and the way it slides down my spine like liquid velvet... undoes me. But I don't have time to process that because he's placing his coat back around my shoulders, drawing me close, rubbing a hand up and down my back.

It takes me a second.

But then I realize he'd noticed the shiver and that he's doing something about it.

Wrapping me in his coat.

Warming me.

Looking out for me.

This man who's a stranger.

Tiptoeing to the edge, glancing down in the precipice, searching for answers at the bottom of a cliff.

"I—" Panic climbs up my throat, and I start to come up with some excuse, some reason to draw away from the big, warm chest, even though there's a part of me that wants to stay close, to lean against the strength, to absorb it into my body, but I don't get far.

Because the door slams open again.

Only, it's not Theo barging through, nearly braining me with the wood and glass.

It's...Toby.

And he sees me wrapped up in a jacket that's not mine, wrapped up in a man that's not...him.

Guilt swirls in my belly, but only for a heartbeat before reality hits, thankfully hard enough to snap my mouth shut, cutting off the apology that is bubbling up my throat.

Jesus, Jolie. Get your life together.

There was no way I was apologizing to him.

Not fucking *ever*.

I lift my chin, hear Leo chuckle softly. "That's right, sweetheart."

And seriously, why the fuck does it not bother me that he's calling me that, but his friend calling me the same felt... icky. Hell, even the gentle *honey* from Theo, who was just trying to be nice about the fact that my boyfriend—my *ex*-boyfriend—is a dirtbag, right along with my best friend, had felt a bit yucky.

But Leo's quiet, rasping velvet of *sweetheart*, the soft puffs of his words against the back of my neck feels...right.

Still, I don't have time to process what that means.

Because the look on Toby's face...

Is approaching bulldog.

And that means I'm in for a fight that's going to drain the shit out of me.

Probably why I sigh and snap, "Don't you fucking dare."

He freezes.

Another probably—because I don't snap at him. Not ever. But then again, I don't catch him kissing my best friend every day, do I?

"I saw you," I say, still snapping, my chin lifting further. "I saw you kissing Colleen."

His face blanches, and I know that it's all over—that the tiny bit of hope that's buried deep in my heart is for naught—when his eyes dart to the side and he says, "It's not what you think."

It's exactly what I think.

Which is why it's not a surprise that I see Colleen push the door open.

That I see her gaze hit Toby first.

Longing. Need. No. *Greed.*

For *my* boyfriend.

A hand settles gently on my back, and I find myself leaning into it, into that strength.

"I saw you," I say again, this time to Toby *and* Colleen.

"It's not—"

"I didn't believe you when you said that the first time," I bite out, narrowing my eyes at Toby. "And I don't believe you now." I exhale, shake my head. "In fact, I can't believe you, that either of you—that *both* of you—would do this to me. I—" My throat tightens.

"We didn't mean for it to happen." Colleen now. Making excuses. Bullshitting. Hurting me.

Again.

"If you didn't mean for it to happen, you wouldn't have made out here, with me just going to the bathroom. I was bound to come back and see you guys, but you got off on that, didn't you?" I step closer, leaving the support of that hand. Not needing it. "Because this wasn't the first time." It couldn't be. Not with how comfortable they had looked in each other's arms. Not with how quickly they had locked lips. "You've been doing this other places, haven't you?"

Guilt.

Greed.

That was all I needed to see.

"We're done. *I'm* done." I reach for the door. "With both of you."

FOUR

LEO

I should have moved faster.

That's what I'm thinking when the noise of pain comes, when I realize that her asshole of a boyfriend—*ex*-boyfriend—has moved.

Has grabbed her.

Has grabbed her hand, the one that was injured because of *him*.

Because of that *asshole*.

I'm moving then, before I'm processing actions, getting between them, shoving him back, not giving one fuck when he topples into the bitch former best friend of Jolie's.

"Sweetheart," I whisper, gently cupping her injured hand between both of mine.

"What the fuck do you think—"

I allow my head to whip around, my eyes to meet the ex's.

Allow my deadly intentions to boil up, to show on my face.

I've dropped fuckers twice the size of this asshole on the ice, and I'm itching—*itching* for him to give me a reason to do the same on this snow-covered patio.

Unfortunately, he's a little bitch and he sees that I'm serious (and can back it up), so he just drapes an arm around the asshole ex-friend's shoulders, steadying her.

After hurting the woman he's supposed to love—both emotionally and now physically.

And all over again, I want to punch the fucker.

But...that's not productive.

And not what Jolie needs.

"Come on," I say, shifting so I can tuck her close, can protect her from the assholes outside and the teeming crowd in the bar then tug open the door, guiding Jolie inside.

And if I hit the latch at the top, "accidentally" locking it as we move then it's just that.

An "accident."

But I do make damn sure the door closes all the way.

Let their trek through the icy, half-melted, half-hardened snow to the parking lot be the beginning of their punishment.

Fuckers.

I bustle her forward, pausing at the table of hockey players only long enough to make my goodbyes and exchange narrow-eyed glares with Theo, just for good measure.

Can't let my opponent on the ice become my friend off it.

Even *if* he is a good guy.

Yes, I say that begrudgingly, even in my own head.

Then we're out into the parking lot and the cold is biting at my arms and I'm still bustling, this time to my car, tucking Jolie into the passenger's seat, wondering how long it's going to take for her to realize what I'm doing and get pissed.

The fragile that has surrounded her is again fading.

The strength and fire coming to the forefront.

I just hope I can get her to the hospital first.

"Drive me back, Leo," she snaps. "Right now."

So, I didn't make it to the hospital.

But we're close enough for me to see the sign indicating a turn-in for the emergency room, and I ignore her, pulling into the parking lot and cutting the engine.

I round the hood, tug open her door.

She's still clutching her hand to her chest, even as she's glaring at me, even as she demands, "I mean it. Drive me back to the bar—"

Stubborn fucking woman.

I reach in, unbuckle her belt, wrapping my arm around her middle and guiding her out of the car as I straighten.

There are quite a few perks to being a professional hockey player, I'll admit.

One of those is being in shape, exercising like my life depends on it—and my job does, so my life *does* in a way.

Which means that I have her out of the car in a couple of seconds.

And I have her against my chest in a couple more.

And I'm carrying her toward the hospital doors in just a few additional ones.

Still ignoring her protests.

Then we're inside and I'm walking up to the desk, seeing the receptionist's face change from bland boredom to keen interest as I approach with a protesting woman in my arms.

"She hurt her hand," I say. "It needs an X-ray—"

"I don't need—"

"And for a doctor to look at her. She took a couple of bumps on the dance floor."

"I'm fine—"

To her credit, the receptionist plays along with the scene I'm making. "Her name?"

"Jolie..." I bend, deposit Jolie into the chair in front of the desk and start digging into her purse. Rude, I know, but I'm not going to sit—stand—here and argue for eternity. I retrieve her wallet, pull out her ID.

Glancing at it before I pass it over.

And look at that.

Jolie Levine.

Total rockstar name.

And she's twenty-six.

From Tahoe.

Do I memorize her address before the passing?

Maybe.

But I have the feeling this woman—

She snatches her wallet back with impressive reflexes, considering she's one hand down, and pulls out her health insurance card, glaring up at me. "Do you know how expensive ER copays are?"

"Do *you* know that this is the only place around to get a cast if your hand *is* broken?" I counter, but I tug out my own wallet, snag a credit card and hand it to the registrar. "Can you make sure that the copay goes on this?"

Jolie's eyes flash. "I—" A sigh. "I wasn't asking you to do that."

"I know." I brush back a strand of long brown hair, corralling it with the rest of her half-tamed curls. Then, because her expression is so forlorn, I tug the piece of hair. "Consider this our first date. I'd pay for that, right?"

"Really?" she asks dryly. But her mouth is tipping up at the edges.

I'm making her smile.

Victory is mine!

Also, keeping *that* thought in my head because I need to maintain my cool factor.

My victory is short-lived though. Because her smile fades as she glances over at the woman on the other side of the desk. "I haven't had a guy pay for a first date in...*ever*." A tap to her bottom lip. "Have you?"

The other woman makes a face. "Nope." Then her face clears, mouth tipping up. "Though, I can't say that's completely true. I've had *one* man pay for the first date." She holds up her hand, showing off a glimmering diamond. "And he ended up as my husband."

For some reason, I glance down, my heart pounding...

To find Jolie staring up at me, eyes wide and color high. "I—"

The door to the waiting room opens with a loud *click* that has our gazes jumping apart, has me realizing that we've been staring for who knows how long. Long enough that the registrar has stepped away and my credit card is sitting on the counter and...

A nurse is standing in the open door. "Jolie?" she calls.

Even though the waiting room is empty.

Even though it's just us there.

Even though it's just us in the universe, the only two people on the planet, the only—

Obviously not, dipshit. Considering the nurse is watching us with her brows raised, waiting for us to move.

So she can take care of Jolie.

So she can take away Jolie's pain.

I. Am. A. Total. Dipshit.

I back away from the chair, give Jolie some space so she can get up and walk to the open door.

Then I do something else in a long line of probably shouldn'ts.

I follow her.

FIVE

Wielding a curling iron and pins and blow-dryer while wearing a cast isn't easy.

But I'm doing it.

Just like I absorbed the news of the broken bone in my hand the night before.

Like I accepted Leo standing next to the bed I was in while the doctor delivered that fun bit of information.

Like I dealt with him driving me home, calling a friend on the way to come and retrieve my keys so they could bring my car back to my place.

I'm *not* absorbing the fact that I've finally processed who he is, though.

A member of the Sierra hockey team.

The billboard just outside of town limits showing him posing with Lake Jordan in the emerald green, Tahoe blue, and white jerseys, holding sticks, smiling.

Looking gorgeous.

As gorgeous as he did up close, hair a bit unruly, jaw covered in thick black bristles, lips kissable and showcasing all the teeth in his mouth.

I don't know a lot about hockey.

Just that there's fighting and blood and missing teeth.

And the players are big.

Well, Leo certainly is.

Towering over me, lifting me like I weigh nothing, shoving Toby back like *he* weighs nothing—

Toby.

Shit.

My throat immediately seizes up, pain that I was pretending to ignore, pretending didn't exist, flooding forward.

I exhale, focus on the client in front of me, still together enough that I'm able to comment and nod and smile at all the right places in her story, even with my hand aching and it taking the majority of my attention to not burn her or me or her hair with the curling rod.

I'm a professional, though.

So, I succeed.

In pretending to listen and not burning anything *and* taking her payment.

Thank God for the first two (though especially *number two*), because she's a good tipper, and she's added a Christmas bonus to the amount, along with a card bearing a picture of her adorable new pug puppy. Something she hands me with a hug before disappearing through the door.

Leaving me alone.

In my quiet salon.

My salon.

Another reason I work so hard. Because I've dreamed of this. My place. My name on the door. My clients walking through it.

I'll do anything to keep it.

Sighing, I slump down in the chair and ignore the ache in my hand.

It's too soon for more ibuprofen, and I don't want to take anything stronger until I'm home and don't need to drive anywhere and can get into my jammies and sleep for a billion hours.

But I have to get up first.

Have to get to my car and—

A chime from the bell above the door as it swings open.

"I'm cl—"

But then I look up and see...

"Fuck," I whisper.

Colleen and Toby stand just inside the threshold...their hands interlaced.

Are they fucking kidding me?

I push out of my chair. "What the fuck?" I snap.

Which...not the most articulate. But also...*what the fuck?*

Toby—who'd rarely, if ever, heard such a tone from me—rocks back on his heels. Colleen—who *has* heard that tone, albeit still rarely, but we've been friends since childhood, so naturally she's had more opportunity—just lifts her chin.

Telling me silently that this is the way it is.

Toby is the first one to try to break the news out loud to me. "Jolie, I—"

"Save it," I snap. "You're together. You didn't make a mistake. You want to be together and I just need to deal, am I right?"

I can see exactly where this conversation is going.

In fact, embarrassingly, I've had similar ones with each of them, too many times to count. *This is the way things are going to be. Deal with it.*

But, fuck that.

I'm not going to *deal*.

I'm going—

"Get out," I say, moving toward them and yanking open the door. "I'm done with both of you."

Toby's brows drag together. "Sweetheart—"

I scowl. "Not your sweetheart. Not your girlfriend." I glance over at Colleen. "Not your friend."

Her eyes narrow.

"Not. *Your*. Friend," I say again.

Done. I am *done*.

"I'll box up your shit and leave it on my porch," I tell them. "But I don't ever want to see you again." I jiggle the door, setting the bell off again. "Have a nice life. You deserve each other."

Cheating is a line that—once crossed—cannot be uncrossed.

Cheating between my boyfriend and my best friend.

Well, they are officially dead to me.

Something that seems to shock them. Because Colleen finally drops Toby's hand and steps close to me, arms out like she's going to hug me.

Again...what the fuck?

I stick my hand out, halting her with my palm to her chest.

She *oofs* out a breath.

"I will say this one more time." I glance from her to Toby. "I don't want to see you—*either* of you—again. Not today. Not next week. Not ever."

"But—"

I start pushing, walking her back until she's outside the salon.

Only then do I look over at Toby again, lift my brows. "Out," I say. "Forever."

Thankfully, he moves, walking through the open door, standing by Colleen.

"Forget—" For a second, they both look hopefully, which is just insanity considering what they'd done, what they're *doing*, but that hope disappears when I go on. "Forget coming to my place," I say, "I'll drop your shit off."

My terms.

My time.

Then I slam and lock the door.

And collapse in a chair as I wait for them to leave.

Which they do. Eventually.

Only then do I finally get to go home, finally get to crawl into bed in my comfy pajamas and drink my hot chocolate.

Only then do I let myself cry.

But never in that crying, in the subsequent deep, *deep* sleep that follows do I think I'm anything but...

Done.

D.O.N.E.

———

I wake up late.

Much later than I planned—though I suppose that means I just tried to take my soliloquy of a billion hours of sleep to heart.

I roll over and rub my aching eyes, feeling that they're swollen, and make myself a promise.

No more tears over them.

And I follow through on this promise as I pack up their stuff, shoving it into two giant boxes—clothes and trinkets, gifts that I don't want, toiletries and random plates. A stuffed toy and a throw blanket.

Keys to their places.

All go into the boxes.

Which go into the back of my car.

I drive to Colleen's place, dump her box on the porch.

Then to Toby's, giving his the same treatment.

Then ice cream—because I just got cheated on—and pancakes with crispy bacon because no time of the day is the wrong time for pancakes and crispy bacon.

Then finally, home.

I stop by, open up my mailbox, and head inside.

But one envelope has me frowning.

My name is scrawled on the front, in big masculine letters in handwriting I don't recognize.

Heart pounding, I tear it open once I'm inside my apartment.

> Sweetheart,
> I wanted to check on you but you weren't home.
> I'm on the road with the guys for a week. Text me and let me know you're good?
>   -Leo

The third sentence has a question mark, but I hear it as a command.

Which is probably what Leo intended.

His number is beneath his name and I sigh, setting the note on the counter. Which is when I realize it's not the only thing in the envelope. Frowning, I pull out...

A ticket to the next Sierra game.

Six

LEO

Fuck, I love hockey.

The speed. The physicality.

The way the puck feels dancing at the end of my stick.

I don't have to think about it. My body. My skating. My stick-handling. It's all an extension of me.

The cold of the ice.

The burn of my muscles.

The way my lungs seize for a second when an opponent tries to check me off the puck.

The sting of my hands when the subsequent slash comes.

But I keep skating, doing it as hard as possible, *working* as hard as possible. Possibly because the woman I'm trying to impress is in the stands.

How do I know this?

We've been texting.

And talking on the phone.

She's funny and sweet and tart and...*sweet*.

And she's coming to the game tonight. Is, in fact, in the stands right now. Hopefully being impressed—

Slam.

The hit comes from the side and slightly behind, crushing me into the boards, making all my breath wheeze out of me, the puck squirt ahead.

Thankfully, Lake is there to bail me out, scooping up the puck and skating hard to the net, showing off his speed and strength while I'm frantically trying to suck in air and feeling like Wylie Coyote trying to get my feet under me so I can skate after him, can actually support the play, and do this thing called... hockey.

Lake doesn't need the support, though.

He's tearing toward the other team's goalie, handling the puck in a way that's both annoying and beautiful and—

He makes a move that should be illegal, dragging the puck on the toe of his stick, bringing it behind him, between his legs, and up into the back of the net—

"Fuck you," I whisper as my skating falters for a heartbeat.

But then I'm smirking, shaking my head, thanking God that Lake's on my team even as I'm skating toward him, wrapping him in a big bear hug.

"Fuck yeah," I tell him, slamming my fist into his back, "you fucking dirty bastard."

Lake shoves me away from him, but he's grinning. "Gotta work on those hands, bud," he tells me over the roar of the crowd before skating toward the bench.

I follow, shaking my head, still smirking.

Knowing I can work twenty-four hours a day every day for the rest of my life, solely on stick-handling, and I will never *ever* have the kind of hands that Lake does.

And I'm good.

In the top third of the league.

Lake is just...better.

One of the best.

The kind of guy who's going to be in the Hall of Fame, whose name will be remembered.

Probably because it's a dumb one.

Right up there with *Toby*.

That thought has my smirk disappearing, amusement fading.

Because Jolie and I have been talking. Because I know she officially broke up with him as well as her best friend, Colleen.

Because I know they've both come by her place a couple of times, trying to get in her good graces.

That bitch, Colleen, even asked Jolie to do her hair.

What the fuck?

Luckily, Jolie is done—very done—and since I spent the last week and half getting to know her via text and talking to her for hours on the phone, this is something I know intimately.

I've been getting to know *her* intimately.

Just not...physically.

Something that will hopefully change.

Because she promised to come to the game, and I enlisted some help to ensure she doesn't escape, muahaha.

Okay fine, it's less evil genius and more one of the guys in the back office I'm friendly with is going to escort her downstairs after the game.

Then I'm going to—

Lake shoves me, and I realize I'm daydreaming on the bench. A dumb thing for a professional athlete to do, a dumb thing for *me* to do as that professional athlete, a dumb thing—

The puck flies toward the bench, nearly taking my head off.

I duck.

A dumb thing as a professional hockey player to do in particular.

That's how people lost teeth or got stitches or broke their eye sockets.

All of which I had already experienced once in my life.

No need to experience those again.

"You gonna get your head in the game sometime tonight?" Lake mutters. "Or are you too busy thinking with your dick?"

The latter.

It's the latter.

But I am not going to admit that.

Not to Lake.

Not with the assholes on the right of him, who'll give me a hard time because they are—the aforementioned—assholes listening in.

"My head's in the game," I mutter. "Or did you miss the fact that I just got the assist on your goal?"

"Is that what getting reamed into the boards is called nowadays?" Lake asks.

"Goals don't have to be pretty," I say, scooting farther down the bench, getting closer to the door, closer to the end that's going to enter the ice unless Coach calls for some different combination of players—something that's not usually done unless we're on a power play or penalty kill or things aren't really working.

Considering that we just went up a goal, I don't think he's going to change line combinations any time soon.

"Fair enough," Lake says, but it's tinged with humor.

Like the fucker knows he caught me thinking about Jolie.

"Fuck you," I tell him.

"Fuck you back," he says, standing and hopping over the boards, the play changing, our teammates jumping onto the bench.

I fumble, left flat-footed, but I make it onto the ice.

And I skate after him.

Fuck if that isn't a familiar feeling.

———

I take the quickest shower in history of all showers and now I'm pacing the hallway next to the elevators.

Waiting.

For Jolie.

And wondering if she isn't going to come.

If she's going to go home and I'm going to be left with text messages, phone calls, and a trip to the ER. Wondering if it's all too soon.

She just broke up with her boyfriend.

And her best friend.

Of course she's not going to want to make a connection with a man she just met, probably on one of the worst days of her life. She's not going to—

The elevator doors open with a ding.

I straighten, crane my neck—

Disappointment flows through me.

Just a security guard.

I smile, step aside since I pretty much bum-rushed the elevator, and start waiting again.

And waiting.

Thinking I'm a dumbass.

Wanting things that make no sense considering I only spent a couple hours in person with this girl, that we exchanged texts and phone calls and that's it—

"Hey."

I freeze, whip around, and Jolie is right in front of me.

Fuck.

She's the most beautiful woman I've ever seen—standing there in a pair of jeans and a Sierra tee, the deep blue color making the silver flecks in her eyes pop. Her hair is a lesson in sin, shining curls tumbling around her face, down her chest.

Simple clothes.

But they cling to her curves...

Her curves.

Which I'm staring at like a fucking pig.

I blink, jerk my gaze up, see that the fragile is there, that it's hiding the steel beneath.

Probably because I'm staring. Like a fucking pig.

"Hey," I say back, the Lothario that I am, realizing she must have come down the stairs.

And then I run out of words.

And go back to staring.

She nibbles at her bottom lip, swallows, and I follow the line of her throat, wanting my mouth there, desperate to *taste* her there.

Then I notice her injured hand.

And the words just burst out of me.

"Can I sign your cast?"

Right as Lake Jordan—underwear model, vodka brand ambassador, and fucking All Star—walks around the corner.

SEVEN

JOLIE

My cast is covered in Sierra autographs.

Pink fiberglass dotted with scribbles of black Sharpie.

Scribbles except for Lake Jordan's signature. His name takes up a good portion of my forearm.

And scribbles except for Lake Jordan's signature and...except for Leo's.

Because he blurted out the question just as Lake came around the corner and then the next minutes were filled with my arm being cradled in a series of big hockey hands as signatures were scrawled over the surface.

First Lake's.

Then about twenty others.

Just not *Leo's*.

Now, though, we're alone. No big hands gently turning my arm and signing my cast. No teammates studying me like I'm a science experiment. In fact, no hockey players in the hall at all. Well, no hockey players aside from Leo.

Who's not studying me like a science experiment.

Instead, he's looking at me like…

My belly flutters.

He's looking at me like he did that night, like…the warmth in his voice when he comforted me and the careful way he held me against him when my world imploded.

"You tired?" he asks softly.

I am.

I worked today and it's still not easy doing hair with a cast on.

But…I'm also not.

Watching him on the ice, rooting for him to score when he had the puck, wincing with each hit he took, worry coursing through me, but also…excitement—all of those have my adrenaline going.

Hockey is exciting.

Having a personal connection to someone on the ice below?

Even more so.

"No," I say as he steps closer, fingers tightening on the Sharpie one of the players put in my hand.

"Wanna go for a drive?"

That's…not what I expected him to say, and yet, it sounds perfect.

Dumb, maybe, to be talking to a man so soon after Toby. Maybe I should be nursing my broken heart, taking a beat, stopping and thinking.

But…I stopped and thought a lot when it came to Toby, when it came to Colleen.

Letting a lot of things slide.

Ignoring what *I* wanted.

So, today, I'm going to do what *I* want.

And that's to see what this thing with Leo is, to take a drive with him, to talk and text and…nod. "Yeah," I murmur. "I'd like that."

The frown on his face—the one that had been there from the moment his teammates descended—disappears and he smiles down at me. "Good."

Then he wraps an arm around me, drawing me gently toward him, bringing his big, warm body against mine, wrapping me in a hug that's...

Well, damn.

The man gives great hug.

I sigh, drop my forehead against his chest.

Weird. Fast. *Right.*

Ultimately, that's what the last week and a half have continuously told me.

That this thing between us is weird and fast and right and intense and—

Right.

Yes, to all of those. But mostly the *right.*

Leo's arms around me. Me breathing in his scent. The warm, fuzzy feeling in my belly.

All of it.

"I missed you," he says.

Weird. Fast. *Right.*

I lean back, touch his jaw lightly, brush over the spot where there's a faint pink scar, wonder for a second what caused it, then I say, "I missed you too."

The smile he gives me...

Warm.

Right.

"Should we take that drive?" I ask.

His arms tighten and for a second, I think we're just going to spend the entire night standing in each other's embrace, but then his hold loosens and he wraps one arm around my shoulders, tucking me against his side.

We walk out of the arena.

We get into his car.

And...we drive.

———

The water laps quietly against the shore, soft slaps of sound that break the quiet of the night. There's snow behind us, piles of white fluffy stuff higher on the beach, the result of another—*unwanted*—deposit from the record-breaking snowfall this winter.

But it's the moon that gets me.

Full and bright and gilding the lake in silver, its reflection stretched into a series of ripples and waves, but no less beautiful than its original brethren overhead.

"You like this," Leo says and I glance up, seeing him watching me.

"Yeah," I murmur. "I don't get much time to do it though."

"Why not?"

I shrug. "Life. Work. Expenses. I told you I opened my salon six months ago"—he nods—"and so it's not just dealing with my normal clients, but all of the other stuff." I sigh then admit the truth, both to myself and Leo, "And Toby and Colleen weren't much for the outdoors."

"What the fuck are they doing up in Tahoe then?" he asks.

That's...a good question.

Because this is the land of hiking and snow and the great outdoors, beaches and clear, blue water. This is the land of bears and trails and—

I laugh, those pieces slotting together in a weird-ass puzzle. "No clue."

Leo's face gentles and he touches a finger to my cheek. "Well, let's make sure you get outside more, yeah? Work is good. It's important and fulfilling. It's just"—he crouches a little so our gazes are aligned—"not everything."

I inhale.

Then let out the breath.

Thinking this man gets me.

After a week and half.

And how long did I waste with Toby?

Too long.

"No," I agree. "It's not everything."

A smile as he takes my hand, draws me forward, and I'm not paying attention to my feet, to my surroundings.

Because his hand is warm and I'm feeling all that *right* in my belly.

In my heart.

So, I don't see the rock.

I trip, flying forward, seeing the ground coming up toward my face.

But just like in the bar, Leo's there, catching me, sweeping me up, holding me close, saving me from busting my face open.

"Sweetheart," he chastises lightly, his arms tight around me, my body pressed to his.

I don't fight his hold.

Being held by him isn't a trial—those strong arms, the steady grip, the warmth and the spicy scent of him, the steady bounces of my body against his hard chest as he walks us forward.

Then sits on a rock overlooking the water and that gorgeous reflection of the moon.

"Did you hurt yourself?" he asks gruffly.

I shake my head.

"This too much?" he asks, still gruff.

I shake my head again. "No."

"I don't mean holding you," he presses.

I still. Release a breath. "I know that," I say softly. "I'm okay." I shrug as well as I'm able to, considering he's still holding me. "Really," I add when he snorts quietly. "I think seeing them in my salon was just the nail in the coffin, the final step toward what would have always been the conclusion.

I'm better off without them. And..." I glance out at the lake again.

"And what, sweetheart?" he asks, smoothing my hair back, making my heart skip.

Sweetheart.

From him.

More *right*.

"And...I'm glad I'm here." A beat. "With you."

His eyes warm, mouth hitching up. "Yeah. Me too, sweetheart."

I shiver.

Not from the cold. But from that smile and that velvet rasp and my body being very close to his.

His arms tighten. "You're cold." He starts to stand.

"No," I say quickly, hands going to his shoulders, pushing down lightly, as though I can make him sit again just from that simple touch.

And maybe I can.

Because he *does* sit, even with my casted hand's push being pathetically weak because it's still healing.

But I'm not focused on that.

Because all at once, I realize our mouths are very close.

My inhale is sharp.

My exhale meets his lips as his mouth presses to mine.

Sparks fly behind my closed lids, brighter than the reflection of the moon on the water, erasing everything except for the feel of his body against mine, his lips guiding mine open, his tongue sliding inside, sensation flooding through me like a dam has suddenly burst.

He's kissing me.

And it feels like this is the first time I've ever had a man's mouth on mine.

I sigh.

So fucking perfect.

Especially, when his hand slides up my back, clenching in my hair, tilting my head back, the little twinge on my scalp making me moan and press closer, nails digging into his shoulders, mouth swallowing his groan, feeling it vibrate against my chest.

Feeling him.

Kissing him.

Wanting him.

Which, unfortunately, is the moment he pulls back, leaving us both breathing heavy, even as his mouth tips up again. "My girl can kiss."

That makes me blush.

And the warm, weird, *right* feeling settles in my belly again.

"You're not so bad yourself," I say, waggling my brows.

He chuckles.

My cheeks hurt, I'm smiling so wide. "Leo?"

"Yeah, sweetheart?"

"Wanna do it again?"

No hesitation.

The man doesn't hesitate for one second.

He bends and kisses me under the moonlight.

Eight

Leo

"Fucking, Lake," I mutter as my snowshoes crunch through the snowbanks, my breath puffing out in little white clouds.

Jolie, walking next to me, her breathing much steadier than mine—even though *I'm* supposed to be the professional athlete—giggles.

She *would*.

Considering the sendoff Lake just gave us.

That's the worst part about playing for the Sierra. South Lake has all the vibes of a small town—especially for those of us who live here year round. Tourists come and go, but...hockey players stick together.

Or at least, that's what my teammate has just threatened as we crunch through the snow, finding the trailhead of the path that leads up from the shore and into the trees. It's not far from the little bar where we love to hang out, tucked away in a quieter corner of the lake and away from most of those pesky tourists.

The ones that pay my salary, since they're a big part of the reason the games are sold out.

That aside, I glare at Lake as he continues busting my balls, calling over his shoulder, pretending to head toward the rental kiosk, "I'll be right there to chaperone you two!"

"If that fucker actually rents snowshoes..." I grumble as I turn back toward the trail.

Jolie giggles again, stepping close enough to lean against my side, mouth curved and tempting, and I give in to the urge...

I kiss that smile, taste her giggles, take advantage of the fact that we're here.

Together.

In the daylight. On an actual date.

As in, we're going to spend some time together, grab a bite to eat (that I'm going to pay for), and then we both have a free evening.

Something that's a freaking miracle.

It's been a week since we sat on this very beach beneath the moonlight, a week since I tasted her for the first time, and aside from me stopping by Jolie's Salon (I applaud her for keeping the name simple) and stealing five minutes between clients with her, most of our time together has been on the phone.

Which is good in a way.

I know about her family and her dreams. I know she's planning to take a vacation to Hawaii in the summer (something I plan to talk my way into). I know that she wants a dog but is worried she's too busy for one, not to mention her condo didn't allow pets.

Something else I'm working on.

Because I have a house.

And a big yard.

With plenty of space for a dog.

But she knows about me too—about my parents and my sisters, about shuttling from team to team until I made my place here with the Sierra. She knows that my favorite time of day is the quiet of night, hours after a game, when the adrenaline is just starting to fade.

She knows *me*.

And I know her.

So, yeah, this date, the first official one we're having—as weird as that feels—is important.

So my teammate saying he's going to join us...as ridiculous as that is, as much as I know he's just busting my balls...I'm still feeling protective of this time.

Okay, *possessive*.

Or maybe it's because the sleeve on Jolie's sweatshirt is pushed up, her bright pink cast on display, and—

Lake's fucking signature dominating the space.

I growl again, just thinking about my annoying ass teammate touching *my* woman, though the razor's edge of my anger is tempered when she giggles again, by the blip of amusement I see in her eyes when I glance up.

"That bad, huh?" she teases, navigating the bumpy terrain easily.

Something I'm concerned about, considering she's doing it with a broken hand.

Not that the cast seems to stop her from doing anything—something I've learned over the last couple of weeks.

Even with my shit schedule.

Even with the crunch time that comes from the playoffs closing in.

Even with all the demands Jolie had on her time, her salon over-booked because Christmas is only a couple of days away.

Thus, we haven't spent a lot of one-on-one time together.

I don't want *Lake Jordan* horning in on *my* time.

Asshole.

Who I have begrudging respect for.

And who I like—I suppose—considering he's one of a

handful of guys focused on the job and not the drama in the locker room or squeezing everything they can get out of their teammates.

The Sierra are competitive.

Formidable enemies on the ice.

But we don't have what it takes to get the Cup.

Ultimately, we're fractured.

And I'm not the one to bring us together.

I have the feeling that Lake has the necessary leadership skills, but he hasn't displayed them anywhere other than the scoreboard yet.

Time will tell.

In the meantime, I'll play my ass off, do my best, and try to make sure my life off the ice is as fulfilled as possible.

Jolie slows down as we reach the top of the hill, the backpack she refused to let me carry bouncing against her back. My ego feels better to see she's breathing a little heavy, but I'm a little annoyed that she refused to let me carry it for her.

Deciding to do something about that, I snag it from her shoulders, guiding it off her back, careful of her cast.

"Leo—"

"What do I have these big shoulders for, if I'm not here to carry stuff?" I sling the bag onto my back, surprised by the weight of it.

She narrows her eyes, but her lips are curved and she keeps moving forward, following the trail and not calling me on my pushy ways. We hike deep into the woods, talking about nothing important—TV shows and where we want to eat dinner—but at the same time, building those important pieces. The connections. The commonalities. The ties that bind us together.

It's cold and getting colder, the air on my cheeks as we move making my skin feel tight, but my body is warm when we finally reach a clearing and pause.

"This is perfect," she says, reaching for the backpack, mock glare on her face as she tugs it down my shoulders.

"Perfect for what?" I ask.

She smiles, shakes her head, and sets the backpack down.

Next thing I know, she's spreading a blanket on the ground, sitting on it, unclipping her snowshoes, and patting the space beside her.

I walk over to her, take off *my* snowshoes, then plunk down next to her. "What's up, sweetheart?" I ask.

"This," she says with a smile, digging into the backpack again and passing me a box wrapped in cheerful Christmas paper.

"I—" My teeth click together.

It's not Christmas. Not for a few days. And...I don't have anything for her.

"What's this?" I ask, stomach sinking.

"An early Christmas present."

"*Sweetheart.*"

She touches my cheek. "Don't get all growly. Just open it."

I *am* feeling growly. Mostly because this has taken me by surprise and I'm the asshole without a gift, but I ignore that feeling, start tearing at the paper.

Revealing...a telescope.

"It's silly," she says quickly. "It's just a kids' toy, but I saw it in town and you mentioned that you like looking at the stars after your games. I thought that maybe—"

My heart convulses hard, and I gently trace my fingers over the writing on the front.

"Maybe," she says again, words still coming in a rush, "you'd want to try it out. I know it's daytime—"

I set the box carefully to the side.

"But you can still see some stuff—I Googled it, I promise— and we're up high enough that you have a clear view of the— *ack!*"

I pounce, rolling us, pinning her back to the blanket, all the lush curves of her beneath me.

I mentioned *one* time about the stars and she bought me...

"Toby is a fucking idiot," I say, leaning down and kissing her with everything in my heart. "Because you're fucking amazing."

She inhales.

I trace that gorgeous mouth, her lips reddened from my kiss. "But," I chastise, "I can't believe you brought me out here when I don't have a present for you."

"Leo," she begins.

I narrow my eyes.

Her mouth quirks and it's a fucking beautiful thing. "You still have time."

I do.

And I am going to make it *epic*.

"But..."

She shifts below me, digging into the pocket of her sweatshirt and I push up, see she's holding something small in my direction.

A Sharpie.

"*This* is all I want for Christmas," she says.

My eyes flick up, catch hers, which are dancing with humor. "What?" I ask.

"Will you sign my cast?" She lifts said fiberglass conglomeration and taps Lake's scrawled out name.

"I think there's room right here."

NINE

JOLIE

His face is beyond gentle.

Like it had been with the telescope.

"How did you know I don't like Lake's name on your cast?" he asks.

My hands go to his chest, resting on the muscles there, "How could I tell you're jealous of Lake Jordan, underwear model?" I tease lightly. "I mean"—I shrug, amusement in my belly at his grumpy expression—"I *just* admired his abs on a billboard on the way to meet you." Another shrug. "And then he invited himself to come with us—"

Leo growls.

I grin, lean a little closer, until our mouths are almost pressing together, until our breaths are mingling. "Sign my cast, baby," I murmur.

A nip to my bottom lip, but then he leans back, propping himself up on his knees as he takes long moments signing his name—and doing it in a way that Lake's is completely obliterated...or at least it's mostly illegible.

"There," he says, mouth quirking as he caps the Sharpie. "Merry Christmas."

I laugh, and his face gentles again, that soft, soft voice that has toddlers bouncing around my belly making an appearance when he murmurs, "Beautiful."

God, I like him.

So *freaking* much.

"What?" he asks.

"I like you," I blurt, speaking my thoughts aloud. "So freaking much." Then I clamp my mouth together, feeling like an idiot, considering this is date one and we've known each other for just a few weeks—

"Sweetheart." He brushes his lips over mine. "I've been trying to figure out how to convince you to move in with me so you can get a puppy."

I suck in a breath so quickly I choke.

Then I force myself to take another one, slower and deeper without the side of choking.

"So you're not alone in the liking"—he touches a fingertip to my cheek, the spot that feels hot and is probably bright red— "or in the *so freaking much.*"

"Leo," I whisper.

"I know," he says. "We're going to take our time, enjoy ourselves, but know that's there, sweetheart. The liking." He bends over me again, our lips brushing as he speaks. "And the puppy."

My heart skips, and I find myself wrapping my arms around his shoulders, tugging him down so his body is flush with mine, so his mouth isn't just brushing, but it's pressing, lips parting, tongue thrusting into my mouth.

He groans and I think...

I like him so freaking much.

So...fuck it.

Fuck *him*.

My leg comes up and I wrap it around his waist, grinding against him.

"Jolie," he rasps.

I freaking like *that* too.

Almost as much as I like him skating his hand up my side, dipping under my sweatshirt, diving beneath my sweater and the thermal I'm wearing beneath.

Because his palm on my skin...much better.

In fact, it's so good, I don't feel the bite of winter's air on my skin, don't see the snow on the trees surrounding us.

I just feel Leo and his body and his hands and lips and tongue.

I don't protest when my sweatshirt is tugged up and over my head. I just tear his off as well. And when my sweater and thermal and bra join it, I make sure his shirt lands in the pile. Then his mouth is on my skin, trailing down my throat, latching onto my nipple. He cups the other, massaging it with just the right amount of rough and careful, soaking my panties.

"Shit," he whispers, releasing my breast and sliding his hand across my belly, flicking open the button on my jeans. "This is a bad idea."

His fingers were dipping beneath the fabric of my underwear, so I wasn't in agreement. "No one's around."

He lifts his head, studies the clearing, seeming to listen for several long moments.

For long enough that I hold my breath, not wanting my huffing to influence anything.

Then he glances back at me, eyes hot, and my belly melts.

I know that look.

I know it even as his hand moves, shoving my jeans down to my ankles, my underwear tangled in the denim.

Cold on my thighs and then in between as he spreads them as much as the material allows.

My breath catches when his mouth and fingers get to work, parting my folds as he leans in and suckles at my clit.

"Leo!"

He doesn't stop, thank fuck. Just keeps licking and stroking and driving toward an orgasm that's...

Here.

I cry out, pleasure filling every cell to bursting, spreading out to my limbs, slackening them, weighing me down, hanging heavy on my lids, but I'm not so out of it as to not recognize him reaching for my pants, starting to draw them back up my legs.

I catch him, halting the movements. "What are you doing?" I ask, accomplishing the herculean task of peeling open my eyes.

"You're a little indisposed, sweetheart," he murmurs.

"And you're not indisposed *enough*," I tell him, reaching for the button on his jeans. Tugging down the zipper.

Wow.

That's just...wow.

Something I think I say aloud because his rough chuckle fills the air.

But then I'm wrapping my fingers around him and it turns into a grunt. Then a groan as I start stroking the silken steel.

"Sweetheart—"

I grip tight. Stroke faster.

"Jolie—"

I shiver, heat blossoming between my thighs again.

A bead of moisture on the head of his cock.

I rub it into his skin, feel his body start trembling...

And then I reach for the backpack, for what I tucked into the front pocket before I left my apartment. I'm a former Girl Scout. I'm always prepared.

I get my fingers into the opening, tug the condom out, and hand it up to him.

He freezes, but only for a heartbeat.

I rub yet another bead of moisture into his skin, my thighs

are parted as much as they're able with my jeans still bunched around my ankles, and my fingers are wrapped tight around his cock.

"Hurry, baby."

Then he's opening the packet, tossing the plastic square to the blanket, batting my hands away and rolling the condom down the length of his erection.

Shoving his jeans down farther.

Positioning himself between my thighs, the head of his cock brushing once, twice—

Inside.

I gasp and he pauses, just for a moment, just to let me catch my breath before he's slamming home.

Before he's fucking me.

It's not gentle and sweet. It's rough and a bit of a fight with shoes on and jeans bunched up on our legs and our bodies tangling and the risk of sliding off the blanket and ending up in the snow surrounding us as we move together.

But it's fucking perfect.

This is just us.

Seizing this moment.

Together beneath the sky and amongst the trees, soft words and straightforward touches.

This is just us racing toward completion.

Together.

This is just us...

Flying over the edge, Leo's name on my tongue, my name in the air, pleasure flowing and joy for being in this moment filling us.

Fast. Weird. *Right.*

Us.

I grin as I try to slow my heart, my body sweaty and languid, two orgasms nearly having killed me.

What a way to go.

"Maybe *that's* my Christmas present," I say lightly, when I'm able to speak again without threat of passing out.

Leo grunts, but he pulls me a little closer, lips brushing the top of my ear.

I sigh, burrow back against him, against his warmth, the cold air slowly creeping in, reminding me of exactly where we are.

As though sensing that, Leo kisses me again and sits up, taking care of the condom while teasing me gently when I reveal my Girl Scout preparedness means I also packed tissues and a Ziplock, then buttons up.

A second later, I'm on my feet, my jeans being dragged over my thighs, his fingers working on the zipper, the button.

Bra and thermal on.

Sweater over my head.

Sweatshirt tugged down onto my torso while Leo zips up the backpack.

Snowshoes on our feet and he's just finished tightening the last strap on his when—

Roar.

We both freeze for a second, the sound not processing.

Because it shouldn't be here.

Because...it's fucking *winter.*

And bears are supposed to be freaking hibernating.

ROAR!

Accompanied by breaking branches and crunching snow and—

We look at each other, and Leo tosses the backpack over his shoulder.

The crunching gets closer.

But he's already snagged my hand.

And we're running...

Just as a shadow reaches the edge of the tree line.

TEN

LEO

A bear.

A *fucking* bear.

"Fucking shit," I growl, scooping Jolie up when she stumbles and increasing my speed, taking us between the trees, the rocks and the roots, the piles of snow, the ice and pine needles.

Running as fast as I can in the fucking snowshoes.

Which aren't conducive to speed.

A fucking *bear?*

Seriously?

Something I can't focus on since I'm concentrating on running in the clown shoes, on not dropping Jolie, not leaving her behind to become bear food.

I like her.

I kind of wanna keep her.

So, I keep running, down the path, moving significantly faster than we did coming up. Somehow managing to not trip and fall and break our fucking necks.

Or trip and fall and leave us as bear fodder.

Or—

I burst out onto the beach, skidding to a stop, body tensing as I pivot around, searching the trees for any sign of a lumbering black bear.

A pissed bear who we presumably disturbed from a winter slumber.

What the fuck?

Were we really that loud? To wake a fucking hibernating bear?

"I think we're good," Jolie says, smoothing her uninjured hand over my chest, resting it on the side of my neck. "You can put me down now."

I take one more look then set her carefully on her feet, steadying her as she finds her balance.

"Thanks for not leaving me behind," she says.

I grin over at her, chest heaving, hands dropping onto my knees. "You're tiny. You wouldn't make much of a snack for a bear." I shrug, sucking in a breath, releasing it slowly so as to steady my pulse. "No point in leaving you behind."

Her smile—damn, it's pretty.

"Brutal," she says, and, God, I love seeing her like this, sparks of humor and spice, happiness and good humor, all without one sign of fragile. Just Jolie. Lucky fucking me. "But smart." She moves close, our snowshoes bumping as she stretches up and kisses me. "I like it."

"I like—"

Crunching behind us has us jumping and whipping around.

My pulse is in my throat, racing like a fucking locomotive...

Until I see Lake, goofy grin on his face, snowshoes dangling from his hands as he makes his way toward us.

"I fancied a hike," he calls out.

"Fucking hell," I growl.

Jolie leans against me, mouth twitching. "Should we send him up our trail?"

"He deserves it," I say. "The shit stirrer." I scowl. "But the team needs him to keep putting points on the scoresheet."

Jolie huffs out a laugh. "And *I*—and the rest of the populace—need him to continue gracing billboards."

I glare down at her. "Really?"

She just grins up at me. No fragile in sight.

We were just chased by a bear, and she's laughing at me, grinning as she gives me a hard time. After surprising me with a thoughtful gift...and giving me an orgasm that—

Yeah, the bear was worth it.

But still, "Is this where I point out, I'm on a billboard too?"

She stretches up again, lips brushing my cheek. "Yeah, baby, this is the point where you can say that." Her lips hit my ear. "And I can vouch for your abs being as nice as his."

Damn right they are.

We bend over, unstrap our snowshoes, and I take both sets in one hand.

The snow and sand are mixing here and it's easier to just walk the rest of the way back to the car.

"Lake, just so we're clear," she says without preamble as my teammate comes up beside us, "I'm not into thruples."

I blink.

Lake blinks.

She giggles. "And now that I've shocked two big, tough hockey players"—she takes my free hand and draws me forward—"Lake, feel free to hike away, but not on *that* trail unless you want to disturb a hopefully hibernating bear—"

"*Hopefully* hibernating?" Lake asks.

"Leo, baby." A tug. "We've worked up my appetite"—she glances at me, winks—"let's go eat."

Then she starts forward, towing me along, leaving a gaping Lake behind.

My smile is so wide my fucking face hurts, and I probably look like an idiot.

But I can't bring myself to care.

Not with this woman glancing back, gaze hitting mine, her pretty gray eyes sparkling with humor, her mouth curving and kissable, her fingers tight in mine. "Leo?" she asks.

I pick up my pace, match our strides. "Yeah, sweetheart?"

"I know what I want for Christmas."

"What's that?"

She hesitates for a moment, gaze going to the clear sky overhead, cold sunshine on her skin, turning it golden.

Then she glances back up at me, mouth tipping up at the edges.

"Will you go on a second date with me?"

My lips drop open, and I almost miss the mischief in her eyes.

But I don't as she adds, "Minus the side of bears."

God, I freaking *like* this woman.

Especially, when she laughs as I tease back, "Perfect, because I don't have enough wrapping paper for that."

Especially, as she brushes her lips over mine again.

Especially, as she drops back down to the soles of her feet, takes my hand again, and we walk down the beach.

Together.

Christmas magic in the air.

A future in the sky above.

And sleeping bears sheltered in the trees.

———

Thank you for reading! I hope you loved Jolie and Leo as much as I do! Stay tuned for more of their story in a later Sierra Hockey book. Meanwhile, are you ready to meet Lake Jordan, star forward for the Sierra, underwear model, date crasher, and the man everyone hates to play against? Lake's book, **OVER THE LINE** (https://books2read.com/OvertheLineEF), is coming this November!

I'm snowed in...with a famous hockey player.

My life has been a disaster. I've lost my job, my apartment, and my direction, so when my best friend suggests a week trip up to her house in Tahoe, I jump on the chance for a change in scenery.

Only, I didn't anticipate Snowmageddon.

I didn't anticipate being trapped on the side of the road and rescued by a famous hockey player—and certainly not by Lake Jordan, star center for the Sierra Hockey team, model, and entrepreneur.

I didn't anticipate having to share his house.

Or that there would only be one bedroom.

And I didn't anticipate...that he might want to keep me.

Forever.

CLICK HERE TO GET OVER THE LINE (https://books2read.com/OvertheLineEF) NOW>

———

If you enjoy my stories, considering supporting me on PATREON (https://www.patreon.com/EliseFaber)! Get access to early releases, bonus content, character art, audiobooks, special edition covers, swag, and much more!

———

Hate missing Elise's new releases? Love contests, exclusive excerpts and giveaways? Then signup for Elise's newsletter here! www.elisefaber.com/newsletter

———

And join Elise's fan group, the Fabinators (https://www.face-book.com/groups/fabinators) for insider information, sneak peaks at new releases, and fun freebies! Hope to see you there!

SIERRA HOCKEY SERIES

Also by Elise Faber

Boldly

Breathless

Ballsy

Bewitched

Blowout

Breathe

Blazed

Sierra Hockey Series

Over the Line

Snowed

Caught from Behind

On the Fly

The Big Skate

Rush Hockey Trilogy #1

Big Puck Energy

Filthy Puckboy

So Pucking Over It

Rush Hockey Trilogy #2

Love, Pucks, and Other Stories

All's Fair in Pucks and War

No Pucks Lost Between Us

Rush Hockey Trilogy #3

Puck and Make Up

Blinded By Pucks

Match Made in Pucks

Eagles Hockey Series (all stand alone)

Broken Laces

Knotted Laces

Lace 'em Up

Sinful Bosses (all stand alone)

Ruthless Billionaire

Billionaire's Club (all stand alone)

Bad Night Stand

Bad Breakup

Bad Husband

Bad Hookup

Bad Divorce

Bad Fiancé

Bad Boyfriend

Bad Blind Date

Bad Wedding

Bad Engagement

Bad Bridesmaid

Bad Swipe

Bad Girlfriend

Bad Best Friend

Bad Rebound

Bad Romance

Bad Business

Bad Billionaire's Quickies

Love, Action, Camera (all stand alone)

Dotted Line

Action Shot

Close-Up

End Scene

Meet Cute

Love After Midnight (all stand alone)

Rum And Notes

Virgin Daiquiri

On The Rocks

Sex On The Seats

Life Sucks Series

Train Wreck

Hot Mess

Dumpster Fire

Clusterf*@k

FUBAR

Perfect Storm

Free Fall

Lost Cause

Roosevelt Ranch Series (all stand alone, series complete)

Disaster at Roosevelt Ranch

Heartbreak at Roosevelt Ranch

Collision at Roosevelt Ranch

Regret at Roosevelt Ranch

Desire at Roosevelt Ranch

Phoenix Series (read in order)

Phoenix Rising

Dark Phoenix

Phoenix Freed

Phoenix: LexTal Chronicles (rereleasing soon, stand alone, Phoenix world)

From Ashes

In Flames

To Smoke

KTS Series (all stand alone, series complete)

Riding The Edge

Crossing The Line

Leveling The Field

Scorching The Earth

Cocky Heroes World

Tattooed Troublemaker

About the Author

USA Today bestselling author, Elise Faber, loves chocolate, Star Wars, Harry Potter, and hockey (the order depending on the day and how well her team -- the Sharks! -- are playing). She and her husband also play as much hockey as they can squeeze into their schedules, so much so that their typical date night is spent on the ice. Elise is the mom to two exuberant boys and lives in Northern California. Connect with her in her Facebook group, the Fabinators or find more information about her books at www.elisefaber.com.

f facebook.com/elisefaberauthor

a amazon.com/author/elisefaber

BB bookbub.com/profile/elise-faber

O instagram.com/elisefaber

d tiktok.com/@elisefaberauthor

g goodreads.com/elisefaber